I0817227

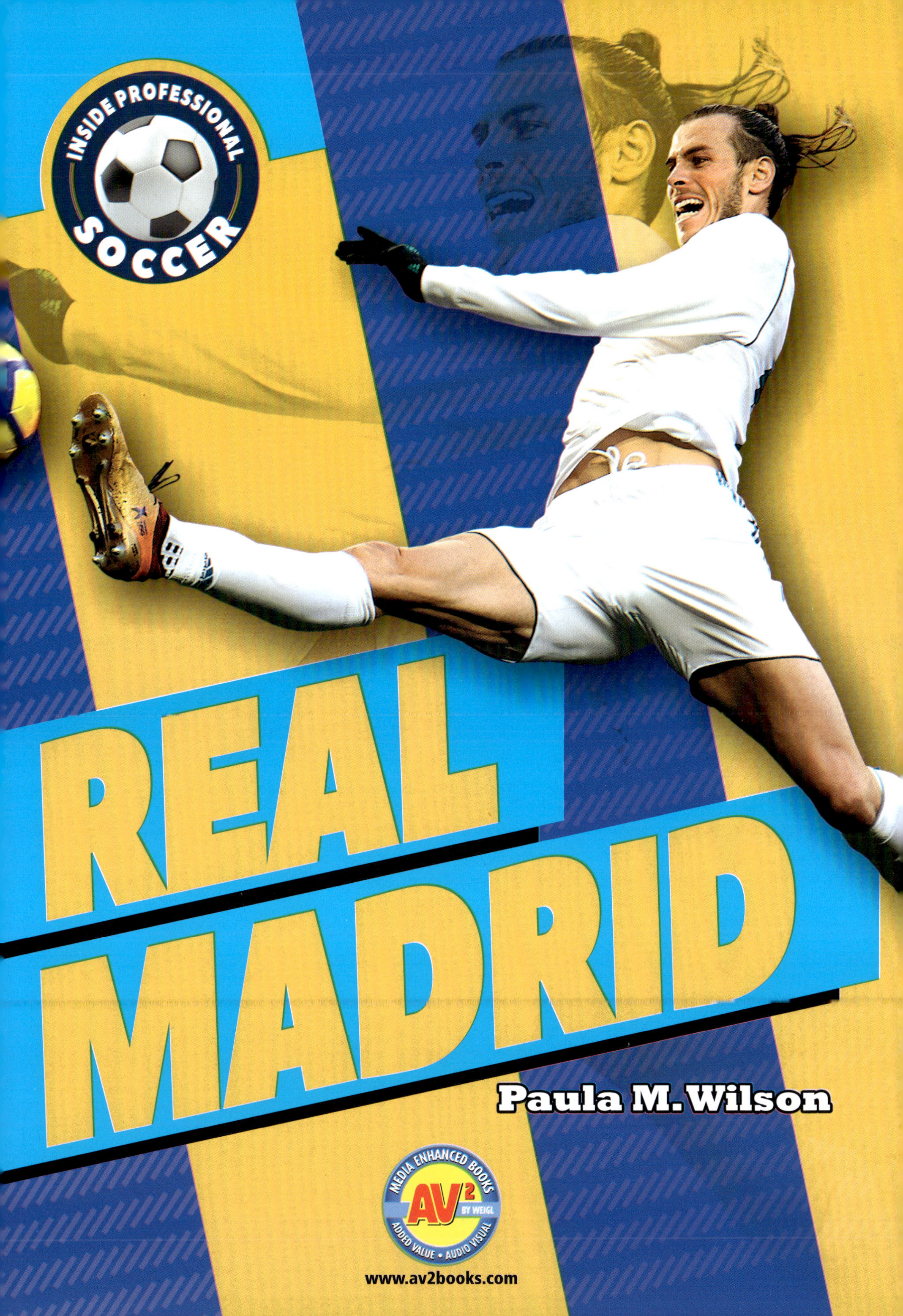
INSIDE PROFESSIONAL
SOCCER
REAL
MADRID
Paula M. Wilson
MEDIA ENHANCED BOOKS
AV2
BY WEIGL
ADDED VALUE • AUDIO VISUAL
www.av2books.com

Go to www.av2books.com, and enter this book's unique code.

BOOK CODE

AVE84679

AV² by Weigl brings you media enhanced books that support active learning.

AV² provides enriched content that supplements and complements this book. Weigl's AV² books strive to create inspired learning and engage young minds in a total learning experience.

Your AV² Media Enhanced books come alive with...

Audio
Listen to sections of the book read aloud.

Key Words
Study vocabulary, and complete a matching word activity.

Video
Watch informative video clips.

Quizzes
Test your knowledge.

Embedded Weblinks
Gain additional information for research.

Slide Show
View images and captions, and prepare a presentation.

Try This!
Complete activities and hands-on experiments.

... and much, much more!

Published by AV² by Weigl
350 5th Avenue, 59th Floor
New York, NY 10118
Website: www.av2books.com

Library of Congress Control Number: 2018930406

ISBN 978-1-4896-7770-9 (hardcover)
ISBN 978-1-4896-7771-6 (softcover)
ISBN 978-1-4896-7772-3 (multi-user eBook)

Printed in the United States of America in Brainerd, Minnesota
1 2 3 4 5 6 7 8 9 0 22 21 20 19 18

022018
120817

Project Coordinator: John Willis   Designer: Terry Paulhus

The publisher acknowledges Getty Images, Alamy, and Wikimedia as its primary image suppliers for this title.

CONTENTS

Introduction

Real Madrid Club de Fútbol has dominated the Spanish soccer league for decades. Soccer is primarily known as football in many European countries. Many people consider Real Madrid one of the greatest soccer teams in the world. The team is located in Madrid, Spain's capital city. They have brought home more Spanish league championship titles than any other team in history. Their success extends past Spain's border as well. They have won more than 15 European titles and **cups**.

At the 2016 UEFA Champions League Final, Real Madrid beat Atlético Madrid with penalty kicks. The final score was 5–3.

Their legacy as a **powerhouse** club stretches back for generations. There is no sign that their dominance is slowing down. The squad has fielded some of the biggest and best names in the sport. These include Alfredo Di Stéfano, David Beckham, Kaká, Zinedine Zidane, and current superstar Cristiano Ronaldo, who continues to shatter one record after another.

Former player and current coach Zinedine Zidane was a big part of Real Madrid's success during the early 2000s.

REAL MADRID

Arena Santiago Bernabéu Stadium

Division La Liga

Head Coach Zinedine Zidane

Location Madrid, Spain

FIFA Club World Cups 6

Nicknames *Los Blancos* ("The Whites"), and *Los Merengues* ("The Meringues")

50 People needed to start an official fan club

3 Intercontinental Cups

11–1 Biggest win

54.7 million Instagram followers

83,329 Record attendance

History

Real Madrid won the European Cup for the sixth time in 1966. They were playing against the Serbian soccer team FK Partizan.

In the late 1800s, soccer's popularity exploded in England and Scotland. Soon after, the sport came to other European countries, including Spain. In 1902, the Madrid Football Club was created.

They went on to win four of the first six Spanish league tournaments, to the disappointment of their rival team, Barcelona. In 1920, King Alfonso XIII of Spain granted the team the right to use the word *real*, meaning "royal," in their name. During the 1950s, 1960s, and 1970s, the Whites dominated the Spanish soccer world, with very few losing seasons. Their success continued into the 21st century with six Spanish league title wins in 17 years.

A strategy that the club created early on is to sign players known as *galácticos*, or "superstars." Through the years, the Whites have invested hundreds of millions of dollars to attract powerhouse players. This strategy seems to be working. In 2000, soccer's official **governing** association, Fédération Internationale de Football Association (FIFA), declared that Real Madrid was the best soccer club of the 20th century.

Santiago Bernabéu was the president of Real Madrid for 33 years. During that time the club won 71 trophies.

The Arena

The Santiago Bernabéu Stadium is not just for soccer. Famous musical acts, such as **U2** and **Bruce Springsteen**, have held concerts there in front of more than **80,000 people**.

Santiago Bernabéu Stadium is the second-largest stadium in the Spanish soccer league, behind Barcelona's Camp Nou stadium's 99,000 seats.

Real Madrid has grown greatly in size and popularity since 1902. At first, they played on a small field next to a bullfighting ring. As soccer grew, the team needed room for **spectators**. They moved to Campo de O'Donnell, where 6,000 fans could watch. Then, in 1924, the team expanded into their very own stadium, called the Chamartín. It had space for 15,000 spectators. However, the team's fans continued to outgrow the stadium space.

In 1943, the team's president was Santiago Bernabéu. He knew the team needed a much larger place to call home. In 1947, his dream became a reality when the new Estadio Chamartín opened with room for 100,000 people. Eight years later, the stadium was renamed the Santiago Bernabéu Stadium as a **tribute** to his dedication to the team.

To prepare for the 1982 World Cup, which took place in Spain, Real Madrid renovated the entire stadium again. They added an electronic scoreboard, better lighting, and a metal roof covering most of the seats. By 2016, plans were again underway to upgrade and remodel the stadium. By 2020, it will feature a removable roof and an updated style.

Fans can tour Santiago Bernabéu Stadium and visit the Best Club in History room. This contains audiovisual and interactive exhibits of the team's history.

Where They Play

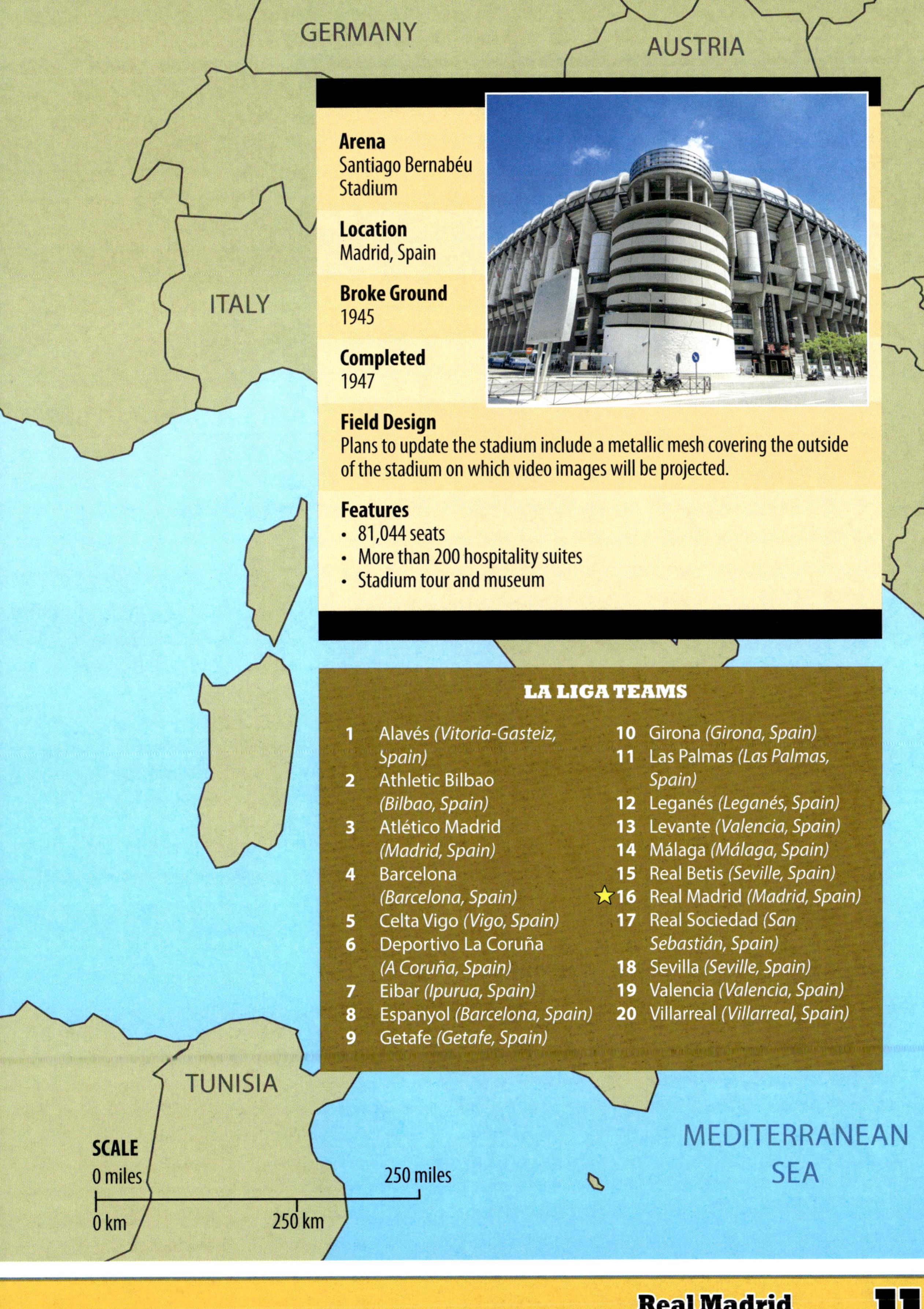

Arena
Santiago Bernabéu Stadium

Location
Madrid, Spain

Broke Ground
1945

Completed
1947

Field Design
Plans to update the stadium include a metallic mesh covering the outside of the stadium on which video images will be projected.

Features
- 81,044 seats
- More than 200 hospitality suites
- Stadium tour and museum

LA LIGA TEAMS

1 Alavés *(Vitoria-Gasteiz, Spain)*
2 Athletic Bilbao *(Bilbao, Spain)*
3 Atlético Madrid *(Madrid, Spain)*
4 Barcelona *(Barcelona, Spain)*
5 Celta Vigo *(Vigo, Spain)*
6 Deportivo La Coruña *(A Coruña, Spain)*
7 Eibar *(Ipurua, Spain)*
8 Espanyol *(Barcelona, Spain)*
9 Getafe *(Getafe, Spain)*
10 Girona *(Girona, Spain)*
11 Las Palmas *(Las Palmas, Spain)*
12 Leganés *(Leganés, Spain)*
13 Levante *(Valencia, Spain)*
14 Málaga *(Málaga, Spain)*
15 Real Betis *(Seville, Spain)*
☆16 Real Madrid *(Madrid, Spain)*
17 Real Sociedad *(San Sebastián, Spain)*
18 Sevilla *(Seville, Spain)*
19 Valencia *(Valencia, Spain)*
20 Villarreal *(Villarreal, Spain)*

The Uniforms

For the 2017–2018 season, the blue trim on the team's white home kit was inspired by the blue sky over Madrid.

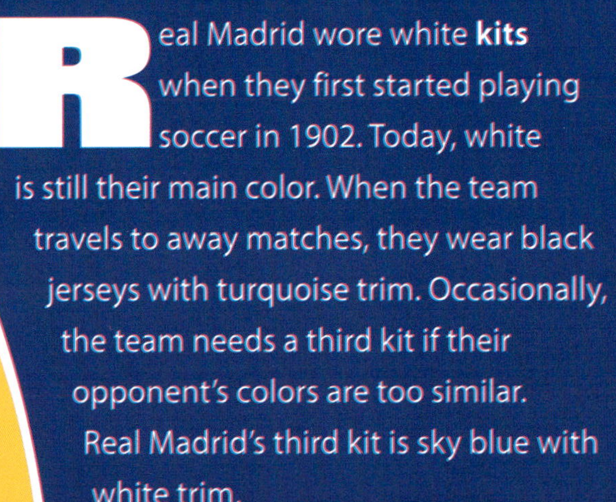

Real Madrid wore white **kits** when they first started playing soccer in 1902. Today, white is still their main color. When the team travels to away matches, they wear black jerseys with turquoise trim. Occasionally, the team needs a third kit if their opponent's colors are too similar. Real Madrid's third kit is sky blue with white trim.

The team logo began as a simple **monogram** of the team letters, MFC, for Madrid Football Club. When the King of Spain granted the team the right to use the word *real*, the logo was updated with a crown and a blue stripe. The stripe represents the region of Castile, where the team is originally from. In 2017, to celebrate their 115 years as a club, the team wore a patch with the years 1902–2017 printed at the bottom of their shirts.

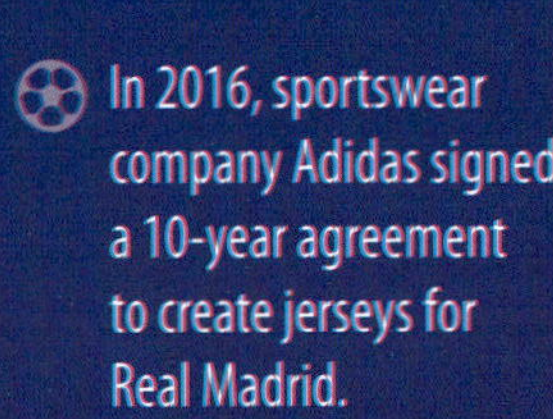

In 2016, sportswear company Adidas signed a 10-year agreement to create jerseys for Real Madrid.

Goalie Gear

Before signing with Real Madrid, Keylor Navas played for Albacete in Spain.

You can always pick out the **goalkeepers** in soccer because they wear a different-colored jersey from their teammates. Instead of wearing white shirts, Real Madrid goalkeepers wear a solid color. This color has changed over the years. Recently, bright red or forest green are the colors of choice for Real Madrid keepers.

Unlike other professional sports goalies, most soccer keepers do not wear any special body padding or helmets. However, they are allowed to wear gloves to protect their hands. The gloves also provide additional grip when handling the ball.

Since 2014, Real Madrid fans have cheered on Keylor Navas, the squad's 6 foot (183 centimeter) goalkeeper from Costa Rica. Navas's quick reflexes and ability to protect the Real Madrid goal have helped the team win one Spanish League championship and two UEFA Champions League titles (called the European Cup until 1992). In 2017, Navas was a runner-up for the Best FIFA Goalkeeper award.

Since joining the team, Keylor Navas has helped the Whites bring home several titles, including three FIFA Club World Cups.

The Coaches

In 2017, Zinedine Zidane received the Best FIFA Men's Coach award.

Zinedine Zidane played for Real Madrid for five years, helping them win the Spanish league championship in 2003.

Real Madrid has had more than 50 coaches since the team was formed. Some coaches only stayed with the team for a year or two. Others, such as Vicente del Bosque, led Real Madrid for multiple seasons. Miguel Muñoz served the team the longest, for 15 years from 1959 to 1974.

VICENTE DEL BOSQUE Before becoming Real Madrid's coach in 1999, Vicente del Bosque was a star player for the Whites during the 1970s. During his playing career, Real Madrid had incredible success. As a calm yet powerful coach, del Bosque led the team to seven trophies. His success as a coach included a league championship in 2000 and again in 2002.

MIGUEL MUÑOZ Miguel Muñoz began his career with Real Madrid as a player in 1948. In 1959, he moved easily into the coaching role. Muñoz built a powerhouse team that dominated the league, winning five straight league championships from 1961 to 1965. Under Muñoz, Real Madrid brought home 14 trophies. These included an amazing total of nine league championships and two European Cups.

CARLO ANCELOTTI Carlo Ancelotti was the coach of the Whites for just two seasons, but his impact was enormous. Under his guidance, the squad won their 10th European Cup during the UEFA Champions League match in a 4–1 victory over Atlético Madrid in May 2014. Ancelotti was also instrumental in signing **standout** talent, including **forward** Gareth Bale, to the team.

Fans Around the World

Real Madrid fans sing and chant to show their support for their team. A fan favorite is *Hala Madrid y Nada Más*, "Go Madrid and Nothing More."

Millions of Real Madrid fans span the globe. People from Indonesia and China to the United States and Canada can be found cheering for the team. Fans, called Madridistas, share their love of the team on social media sites such as Facebook, Twitter, and Instagram. The Real Madrid Facebook page has more than 100 million followers. Forward Cristiano Ronaldo has 120.5 million Facebook followers, one of the highest in the world.

Fans worldwide flock to the Real Madrid **app**, which features highlight reels, player stats, and training videos. Fans using the app can listen to live radio broadcasts of games in either English or Spanish. There is also a magazine called *Hala Madrid*, meaning "Go Madrid," that is printed four times a year.

Fan Traditions

#1 Fans can become official card-carrying members of the Madridistas Club. Benefits include discounts, newsletters, and chances to win tickets and prizes.

#2 Die-hard fans can watch Real Madrid TV, a TV station dedicated to broadcasting live games, interviews, and team news.

Legends of the Past

Many great players have suited up for Real Madrid. A few of them have become icons of the team and the city it represents.

Raúl

Known simply as Raúl, forward Raúl González Blanco made a name for himself on the **pitch** as a natural leader. As team captain, he led the squad to several titles. These included six league championships and three UEFA Champions League titles between 1994 and 2010. Known for his stamina and speed, Raúl set the team record in 2009 for the most goals. The record was later broken in 2015 by Cristiano Ronaldo. Raúl spent 16 years with the Whites before moving on in 2010 to play for Schalke 04, a team in the German professional soccer league.

Position: Forward
Years in Pro Soccer: 1994–2015
Born: June 27, 1977, Madrid, Spain

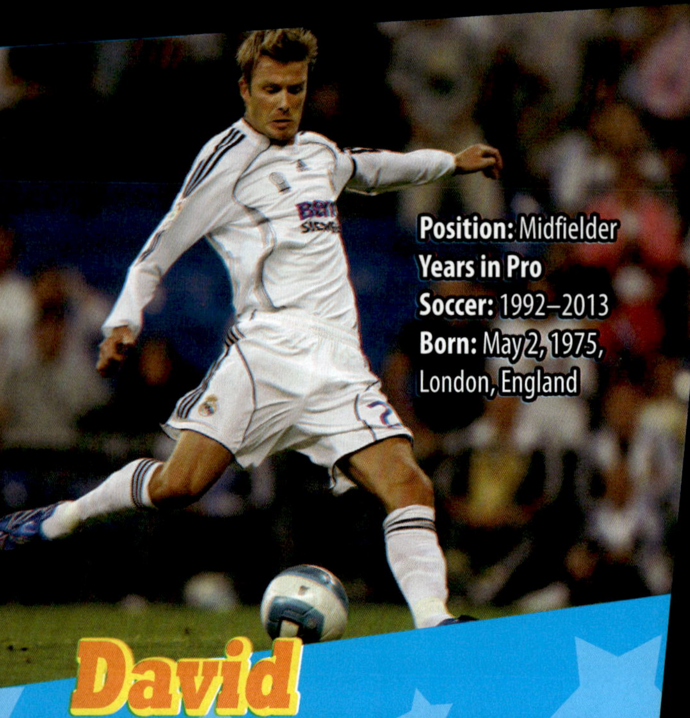

Position: Midfielder
Years in Pro Soccer: 1992–2013
Born: May 2, 1975, London, England

David Beckham

Midfielder David Beckham was known for his passing and kicking precision. Beckham helped the squad win the 2007 league championship 3–1 over RCD Mallorca. The Whites also brought home the Spanish Super Cup that same year. His star power on and off the field has made Beckham a worldwide sensation. In 2007, he made the switch to the United States. He signed with the LA Galaxy, a professional soccer team in Major League Soccer (MLS).

Position: Forward
Years in Pro Soccer: 1944–1966
Born: July 4, 1926, Buenos Aires, Argentina

Alfredo Di Stéfano

Alfredo Di Stéfano is a legend in Real Madrid history. He played for the Whites from 1953 to 1964 and made his mark as one of the best players of all time. Di Stéfano helped the Whites bring home eight league titles, a Spanish Cup, and five European Cups. He led the team in scoring, with 308 goals in 396 appearances. He received the FIFA Ballon d'Or award for being the best player in Europe in 1957 and 1959. Then, in 1989, he was awarded the Super Ballon d'Or, an honor no one else has received. This was an unprecedented tribute to Di Stéfano's domination of the world of soccer.

Ferenc Puskás

Ferenc Puskás played for the Whites from 1958 to 1967. He made his mark as a goal-scoring machine with agility, accuracy, and power. The duo of Puskás and his teammate Alfredo Di Stéfano was unstoppable. They brought Real Madrid five straight Spanish league championships, a record in the league's history. During his time with the team, Puskás also helped bring home three European Cups. In Puskás's nine years with Real Madrid, he scored 242 goals in 262 appearances. Puskás was considered to have the best left foot in team history. The talented forward was the league's top scorer in four seasons. FIFA paid tribute to Puskás by naming their award for the best goal of the year, the FIFA Puskás Award, after him.

Position: Forward
Years in Pro Soccer: 1943–1966
Born: April 2, 1927, Budapest, Hungary

Stars of Today

Today's Real Madrid team is made up of many young, talented players who have proven that they are among the best in the league.

Cristiano Ronaldo

In Cristiano Ronaldo's first season with Madrid, the 6 foot 1 inch (185 cm) forward scored 40 goals. At the time, this was a Spanish league record. Season after season, Ronaldo broke scoring records and helped bring his team to the top of the league standings. With Ronaldo leading, Real Madrid won two league championships, two Spanish Super Cups, and four UEFA Cups. Ronaldo's star power is recognized around the world. He won the FIFA World Player of the Year award five times, most recently in back-to-back seasons in 2016 and 2017.

Position: Forward
Years in Pro Soccer: 2003–present
Born: February 5, 1985, Funchal, Portugal

Marcelo Vieira

Marcelo Vieira joined Real Madrid in 2007 from the Italian soccer league team Fluminense FC. An effective **defender**, the 5 foot 7 inch (174 cm) Marcelo has incredible ball-handling skills and speed. His skills have helped bring the Whites to four Spanish league titles and two Spanish Cups. Real Madrid has also won three UEFA Champions League titles and three UEFA Super Cups with Vieira defending the goal. He also plays for his home country, Brazil, on its national team. He participated in the Beijing 2008 Summer Olympics and the London 2012 Summer Olympics.

Position: Defender
Years in Pro Soccer: 2006–present
Born: May 12, 1988, Rio de Janeiro, Brazil

Gareth Bale

In 2013, Gareth Bale arrived in Madrid. He had previously played on an English Premier League team, Tottenham Hotspur FC. Gareth immediately made his mark on Real Madrid as a powerful forward. His stamina and pace are hard to stop. The 6 foot (185 cm) striker is considered by many to be one of the fastest soccer players in the world. He has helped the Whites to a Spanish league championship, a Spanish Super Cup win, and three each of the UEFA Champions League titles and UEFA Super Cups. Bale also lends his talent to his home country, Wales, on its national team.

Position: Forward
Years in Pro Soccer: 2006–present
Born: July 16, 1989, Cardiff, Wales

Isco

Francisco Román Alarcón Suárez, known as Isco, joined the Whites in 2013. Since then, he has made his mark as a talented attacking midfielder. He has shown that he can easily find his way through any opponent's line of defense. Prior to signing with Real Madrid, Isco played for another Spanish league team, Málaga. Isco's speed and ball-handling skills helped Real Madrid win the Spanish league title, a Spanish Super Cup, three UEFA Champions League titles, and three UEFA Super Cups. Isco has also been a fixture on the Spanish national team since 2012.

Position: Midfielder
Years in Pro Soccer: 2009–present
Born: April 21, 1992,
Benalmádena, Spain

All-Time Records

33
Most League Championships
The Whites have brought home the Spanish league championship a record 33 times. Barcelona is a distant second with 24.

12
Most UEFA Champions League wins
Real Madrid broke the record by winning their 10th UEFA Champions League title in 2014. They added two more to their total in 2016 and 2017.

127
Most Assists
Cristiano Ronaldo is not only the team's top scorer, he also leads the team in assists with a total of 127.

40

Longest Winning Streak

Real Madrid's 2016–2017 squad of superstars reached the 40 unbeaten games mark in the Spanish soccer league, surpassing Barcelona's streak of 39 wins.

741

Most Appearances

Raúl González Blanco played for 16 years with Real Madrid and appeared in 741 matches.

Timeline

Throughout the team's history, Real Madrid has had many memorable events that have become defining moments for the team and its fans.

1902
The Madrid Football Club is established.

1932
The team wins their very first Spanish league championship.

1947
Chamartín Stadium, with room for an amazing 100,000 people, opens with Madrid capturing a 3-1 win over the Portuguese team CF Os Belenenses.

1890 1900 1910 1920 1930 1940 1950

In 1905, the young team wins their first Spanish Cup, then goes on to win three more in a row.

1920
The King of Spain, Alfonso XIII, grants the word *real* to the club. They can now call themselves Real Madrid.

1956
Real Madrid takes home the first European Cup ever played, with a win over France's Stade de Reims. They go on to win four more European Cups in a row.

1964
Real Madrid wins their 10th league championship, led by the powerhouse duo of Alfredo Di Stéfano and Ferenc Puskás.

1982
The Santiago Bernabéu Stadium is renovated to host the 1982 World Cup tournament. Modern lighting and an electronic scoreboard are added to the enormous stadium.

1960 1970 1980 1990 2000 2010 2020

In 1980, the Whites earn their 20th Spanish league championship.

2017
Real Madrid wins the UEFA Champions League and the Spanish league championship in the same year.

The Future
The team has its sights set on winning the "treble." This is when a team wins the league championship, the Spanish Cup, and the UEFA Champions League in one year. Real Madrid has some of the best athletes in the sport and the backing of millions of passionate fans. It looks like Real Madrid may very well reach their goal and sit atop the soccer world for years to come.

Write a Biography

Life Story

A person's life story can be the subject of a book. This kind of book is called a biography. Biographies often describe the lives of people who have achieved great success. These people may be alive today, or they may have lived many years ago. Reading a biography can help you learn more about a great person.

Get the Facts

Use this book, and research in the library and on the internet, to find out more about your favorite player. Learn as much about him as you can. What position does he play? What are his statistics in important categories? Has he set any records? Also, be sure to write down key events in the person's life. What was his childhood like? What has he accomplished off the field? Is there anything else that makes this person special or unusual?

Use the Concept Web

A concept web is a useful research tool. Read the questions in the concept web on the following page. Answer the questions in your notebook. Your answers will help you write a biography.

Concept Web

Write a Biography

Adulthood

- Where does this individual currently reside?
- Does he or she have a family?

Your Opinion

- What did you learn from the books you read in your research?
- Would you suggest these books to others?
- Was anything missing from these books?

Childhood

- Where and when was this person born?
- Describe his or her parents, siblings, and friends.
- Did this person grow up in unusual circumstances?

Accomplishments off the Field

- What is this person's life's work?
- Has he or she received awards or recognition for accomplishments?
- How have this person's accomplishments served others?

Help and Obstacles

- Did this individual have a positive attitude?
- Did he or she receive help from others?
- Did this person have a mentor?
- Did this person face any hardships?
- If so, how were the hardships overcome?

Accomplishments on the Field

- What records does this person hold?
- What key games and plays have defined his career?
- What are his stats in categories important to his position?

Work and Preparation

- What was this person's education?
- What was his or her work experience?
- How does this person work?
- What is the process he or she uses?

Trivia Time

Take this quiz to test your knowledge of Real Madrid. The answers are printed upside down under each question.

1 Who let the team use the word *real* in their name?

A. Spain's King Alfonso XIII

2 When was the team crowned the best soccer team of the 20th century?

A. 2000

3 How many European Cups (or UEFA Champions League titles) has the team won?

A. 12

4 What are Real Madrid fans called?

A. Madridistas

5 Who is the current goalkeeper for the Whites?

A. Keylor Navas

6 How many FIFA World Player of the Year awards does Cristiano Ronaldo have?

A. Five

7 What is Real Madrid's jersey color for home games?

A. White

8 How many people could watch Real Madrid at Campo de O'Donnell?

A. 6,000

9 Where did David Beckham transfer to after playing for Real Madrid?

A. LA Galaxy

Key Words

app: a computer program that performs a special function

cups: trophies, and in some cases, the names of actual competitions

defender: the player on a soccer team whose job it is to stop opponents from scoring

forward: a player on a soccer team who normally plays closest to the opponent's goal

goalkeepers: also called goalies. The players responsible for keeping the ball from going into the goal and the only players who are allowed to pick up the ball.

governing: controlling and making decisions for an organization or group

kits: standard attire and equipment worn by soccer players, including shirts, shorts, socks, and shin guards

midfielder: a player on a soccer team who normally plays in the middle area of the field

monogram: a symbol with two or more letters used as a logo or decoration

pitch: an area that is used for playing sports

powerhouse: a team that has a lot of energy, strength, and skill

spectators: people who watch an event, game, or show

standout: a person or thing that is better or more important than others in a group

tribute: something that is said or given to show respect or affection for someone

Index

Log on to www.av2books.com

AV² by Weigl brings you media enhanced books that support active learning. Go to www.av2books.com, and enter the special code found on page 2 of this book. You will gain access to enriched and enhanced content that supplements and complements this book. Content includes video, audio, weblinks, quizzes, a slide show, and activities.

AV² Online Navigation

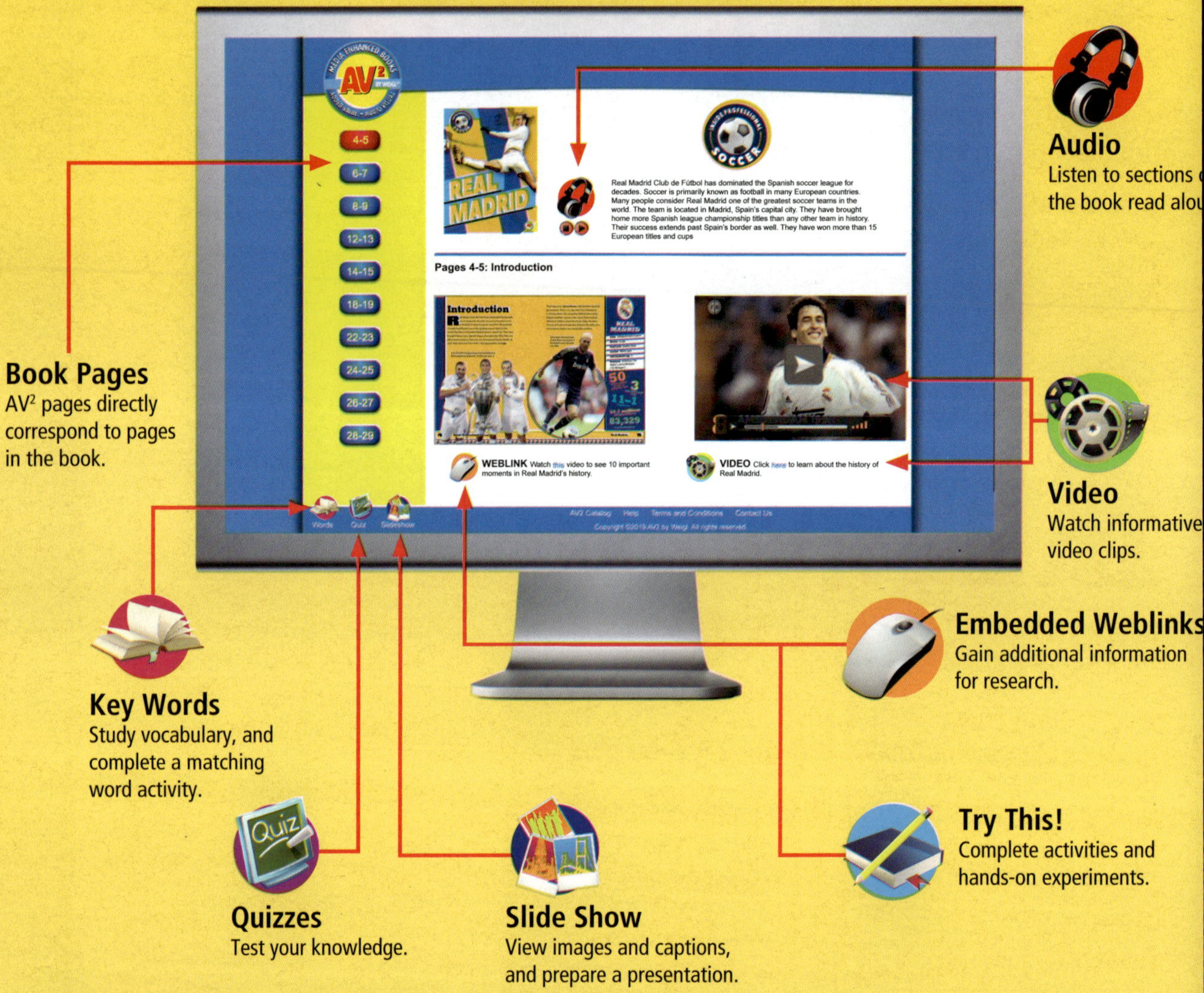

Book Pages
AV² pages directly correspond to pages in the book.

Audio
Listen to sections o
the book read alou

Video
Watch informative
video clips.

Embedded Weblinks
Gain additional information for research.

Key Words
Study vocabulary, and complete a matching word activity.

Try This!
Complete activities and hands-on experiments.

Quizzes
Test your knowledge.

Slide Show
View images and captions, and prepare a presentation.

AV² was built to bridge the gap between print and digital. We encourage you to tell us what you like and what you want to see in the future.

Sign up to be an AV² Ambassador at www.av2books.com/ambassador.

Due to the dynamic nature of the Internet, some of the URLs and activities provided as part of AV² by Weigl may have changed or ceased to exist. AV² by Weigl accepts no responsibility for any such changes. All media enhanced books are regularly monitored to update addresses and sites in a timely manner. Contact AV² by Weigl at 1-866-649-3445 or av2books@weigl.com with any questions, comments, or feedback.